2/9/2019.

D0525304

S OT

Please renew or return items by the date shown on your receipt

www.hertsdirect.org/libraries

Renewals and enquiries: 0300 123 4049

Textphone for hearing or speech impaired   0300 123 4041

Hodder
Children's

520 361 73 8

To Sally

Special thanks to Gill Harvey

Little Animal Ark is a trademark of Working Partners Limited
Text copyright © 2002 Working Partners Limited
Created by Working Partners Limited, London, W6 0QT
Illustrations copyright © 2002 Andy Ellis

First published in Great Britain in 2002 by Hodder Children's Books

This edition published in 2007

A Catalogue record for this book is available from the
British Library

ISBN-13: 978 0 340 93258 2

Printed and bound in Great Britain by
Clays Ltd, St Ives plc

The paper and board used in this paperback by Hodder Children's
Books are natural recyclable products made from wood grown in
sustainable forests. The manufacturing processes conform to the
environmental regulations of the country of origin.

Hodder Children's Books
A division of Hachette Children's Books
338 Euston Road, London NW1 3BH
An Hachette UK Company
www.hachette.co.uk

Chapter One

"Come on, Ben!" called Mandy Hope. "Haven't you finished yet?"

It was lunchtime at Welford Primary School. Mandy went over to the table where her friend Ben Stokes was still eating his sandwiches.

"I don't know how you ate your lunch so fast," said Ben.

"It's because I'm so excited!" Mandy told him with a grin.

"I can't *wait* to see Scott's hamsters!"

Scott was Ben's big brother. He was in Class 6, which had a Pet of the Week lesson every Friday. Someone was allowed to bring their pet to school for the whole class to see. And this afternoon Scott was bringing his hamster, Scrabble, with three of her babies!

"I'm excited too," said Ben, munching on his last sandwich. "Even though I see them every day."

"Lucky you!" Mandy said. Mandy *loved* animals – which was good, because there were always lots of them at home in Animal Ark. Her mum and dad were vets.

Mandy didn't have a pet of her own, but she didn't mind too much – she often got the chance to play with her friends' pets.

At last, Ben finished his lunch. He stood up and smoothed down his spiky hair with his hand.

Mandy grinned. Ben was *always* doing that, because his hair was *always* sticking up!

They headed out to the playground to wait for Scott to arrive.

"There he is!" Mandy shouted. She pointed to a blue car pulling up outside the school gates.

Scott got out of the car. He was carefully carrying a big hamster cage.

"Hi, Scott!" Mandy called. She and Ben ran over to meet him as he walked into the playground. Some of Scott's friends from Class 6 came over too.

Mandy peered inside the cage. The three hamster babies were all cuddled up to their mum, Scrabble. "Oh, they're *lovely*!" Mandy gasped.

Two of the babies had silky golden coats like Scrabble's. Mandy couldn't see the third very well, because he was hidden behind his mum.

"Scrabble had six babies altogether," said Scott. "But the other three have gone to new homes.

They're five weeks old, which means they're old enough to leave their mum."

"Now Scott has to find homes for the other three," added Ben.

Just then, the third baby hamster popped up from behind his mum. Mandy saw that he looked different from the others. His fur wasn't sleek and smooth. It stuck out all over!

"Look at that one!" said a girl from Scott's class. She laughed. "His hair looks like it could do with a good comb!"

Scott smiled and nodded. "I've called him Tufty," he said.

"He looks more like a Scruffy
to me!" joked another boy in
Class 6.

Mandy felt a little bit sorry
for Tufty, because people were
laughing at him. "He's still cute,"
she said, sticking up for him.

9

"Tufty's fur is like his dad's," Scott explained. "The other babies are like Scrabble."

Tufty looked up at everyone with dark, shiny eyes.

"He seems really friendly," Mandy said.

"Tufty's great," agreed Scott. "He's a lot more lively than the others."

Just then, Tufty clambered right over his mum to play with a piece of cardboard. He picked it up between his paws, and started nibbling at it. His whiskers quivered madly as he chewed.

Mandy laughed. "Can I hold him?" she asked Scott.

"OK," Scott said. "But be careful not to let him go."

"I'll help you, Mandy," said Ben. Scott opened the cage door and Ben reached in. He gently lifted Tufty out of the cage, then handed him to Mandy.

Tufty seemed to like being held. His nose twitched as he sniffed Mandy's hand. Mandy smiled. Tufty's whiskers tickled!

"Did it take you long to tame him?" Mandy asked Scott.

"Not very long," said Scott. "All the babies have to get used to people. But Tufty liked being picked up straight away!"

Just then the school bell rang. It was the end of lunchtime.

Mandy smoothed the fluffy fur on Tufty's head. Then she carefully put him back into the cage.

"Tufty's my favourite," said Ben.

"I can see why," Mandy said. "I think he's my favourite, too!"

Chapter Two

"The hamster babies are lovely,
Ben," Mandy said, as they all
went to line up.

"Yes," Ben agreed, but he
sounded sad. "I'll miss them when
we've found new homes for them."
Then he smiled again. "But I'll
still be able to play with Scrabble,
and help look after her."

Mandy and Ben said goodbye
to Scott and his friends, then went

to join the Class 3 line.

Miss Rushton led Class 3 back to their classroom and took the register. "Now," she said, when she'd finished. "It's the end of term next week . . ."

Mandy held her breath. They always did something special at the end of term.

". . . so we're going to have
a pet show," Miss Rushton said
with a smile. "Everyone in
Class 3 who has a pet can bring
it in to school."

"A pet show!" Mandy gasped
happily.

"Can I bring Timmy?" Peter
asked. Timmy was Peter's Cairn
terrier puppy.

"Yes, of course, Peter," said
Miss Rushton. "And Mrs Hope,
Mandy's mum, is coming in to
give out prizes."

Mandy beamed. It would be
fun having her mum at school.
And a pet show was even better
than a Pet of the Week day

because everyone's pets would come to school at once!

"Now, we need some good competition ideas," Miss Rushton went on. "Who can think of one to start us off?"

"Biggest Pet!" Paul Jones called out loudly.

"That's the right sort of idea, Paul," said Miss Rushton. "Now, I'd like everyone to go back to their tables, think of a competition, then write it down." She put a piece of paper on each table.

On the Green Table, Mandy and her friends started to think hard.

"Loudest Pet?" Peter Foster suggested, after a few minutes.

Mandy nodded. Timmy had a very noisy bark sometimes!

"I don't think Miss Rushton would want to give a prize for that," grinned Richard Tanner, who had a cat called Duchess. "How about Softest Coat?"

"But Toto doesn't have a coat at all," said Jill Redfern. Toto was her pet tortoise.

"No, nor does Gertie," said Gary Roberts, who had a pet garter snake.

Mandy frowned. This wasn't so easy after all! Then suddenly she thought of something. "I know," she said. "How about Most Unusual Pet?"

"Hey, that's a great idea," said Richard. "Let's have that!"

"I hope no one else has thought of it," said Jill.

Mandy smiled, and wrote *Most Unusual Pet* on the piece of paper.

Miss Rushton came round to collect everyone's ideas. Then she read them out. "The Yellow Table prize will be for the Waggiest Tail," she began.

Peter's eyes lit up. Timmy had a *very* waggy tail.

"The Red Table prize will be for the Prettiest Pet. And the Blue Table prize will be for the Cleverest Pet," Miss Rushton went on. "Finally, the Green Table prize will be for the Most Unusual Pet."

Mandy sighed happily. She could hardly wait for Pet Day. It was going to be great!

Chapter Three

At home time, Mandy's mum was waiting at the school gate. "Hello, love," she said, as Mandy ran over with Ben.

"Miss Rushton said you're coming to our pet show next week!" said Mandy. She stood on tiptoe to give her mum a hug.

Mrs Hope smiled. "That's right. I'm really looking forward to meeting all your friends' pets."

"You can meet some right now," Mandy said. "Have you seen Scott's hamsters? He brought them into school today."

"No, I haven't seen them," said Mrs Hope.

"They're just coming!" Ben said, pointing across the playground. Scott was walking slowly towards them, carrying the hamster cage.

"Scott, can my mum see your hamsters?" Mandy called.

"Sure!" said Scott.

Mrs Hope leaned down and peered in. All the hamsters were asleep – except Tufty. He looked up and scratched his pink nose with one paw.

Then he jumped on to the wheel and started running.

"He's called Tufty," Ben told Mrs Hope.

"Isn't he lovely?" Mandy said.

"He looks full of beans," agreed Mrs Hope, smiling. She looked at Scott. "Have you got to carry them all the way home?" she asked.

Scott nodded. "Mum's taken the car to work," he said.

"Well, we can give you a lift," Mrs Hope offered.

Scott and Ben looked really pleased, and said thank you.

Then Scott clambered into the front of the Land-rover with the hamster cage and balanced it on his knees.

Mandy and Ben got into the back, and Mrs Hope set off.

Mr Stokes was working in the garden as they drew up outside Ben and Scott's house. He waved and came over. "I hope the hamsters enjoyed their trip!" he joked. "Would you like to come in for some tea or juice?" he asked Mandy and her mum.

Mrs Hope smiled. "I have to get back to Animal Ark," she said. "But maybe Mandy would like to stay."

"Oh, yes please!" Mandy said. She scrambled out of the Land-rover.

"I'll come and pick you up in about an hour," said Mrs Hope.

"Thanks, Mum!" Mandy said.

Scott took the hamster cage into the living-room. "Scrabble usually lives in my bedroom," he explained. "But two people are coming to choose a hamster baby today."

As they were finishing their drinks, the doorbell rang. It was a girl called Jade, who had come to choose a hamster.

Ben and Mandy sat next to the cage while Jade and her mum looked inside. Mandy held her breath. Which baby would she choose?

"Oh! Those two are *so* pretty," said Jade, looking at Tufty's brothers.

Scott let Jade take each of them out of the cage. She stroked their silky coats. One of them nudged her hand with his tiny nose. "I'd like this one, please," she said happily. "I'll call him Sandy."

After Jade had left with Sandy, Mandy and Ben watched Scrabble stuff her cheeks full of sunflower seeds. Tufty started to copy her. Mandy laughed. They looked funny with their cheeks puffed out!

Soon, the doorbell went again. This time it was a boy called Robert. He had come with his dad to choose a hamster.

"That one is an odd-looking

thing," said Robert's dad, pointing at Tufty.

Mandy thought Robert's dad was being unkind. She sneaked a look at Ben.

Ben looked back at her and raised his eyebrows.

Mandy grinned. Ben agreed with her!

"I'll have the other one, please," said Robert.

Scott put the last golden hamster baby into the box that Robert had brought with him.

"There's just you and your mum now, Tufty!" said Ben.

Tufty looked around the cage, sniffing in all the corners.

"Can we take Tufty out of the cage, Scott?" Mandy asked.

"OK," Scott agreed.

Ben lifted Tufty out of the cage and put him on his lap. Tufty looked up at him happily – he had something new to explore! He ran up Ben's T-shirt and scrambled across Ben's shoulder. Then he peered into Ben's ear!

Ben laughed – but then he sighed. "No one else seems to see how great Tufty is," he said.

"Well, at least *we* think he's lovely," said Mandy.

Just then, they heard the front door open and shut again. It was Mrs Stokes, home from work.

"Hello, everyone!" she said, coming into the living-room. "Nice to see you, Mandy. How are the hamsters?"

Scott explained that there was just Tufty left.

"Poor old Tufty," said Mrs Stokes. "He's certainly the odd one out!" Then she looked at Ben and sighed. "Ben, what have you been up to? Your hair's sticking up even more than usual!"

"Just playing with Tufty," said Ben.

Mandy looked at Ben's hair. His mum was right. It was sticking up all over! "Ben, you look just like Tufty!" she joked.

Ben laughed. He tried to smooth his hair down with his hands. But the tufts sprang back up again.

"You know what?" said Scott suddenly. "I think we've found a new owner for Tufty, after all."

Mandy was puzzled. There hadn't been any more visitors.

Ben looked surprised too, and a bit sad. "Are you sure?" he asked.

Scott grinned. "Yes," he said.

"Who is it?" Mandy asked.

"Ben, of course!" said Scott.
"I think Tufty deserves a tufty
owner!"

Chapter Four

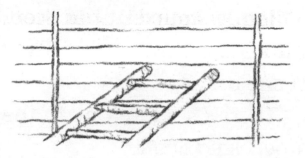

At first, Ben looked surprised.
Then he beamed with delight. He
looked at his mum. "Is that OK,
Mum?" he asked.

Mrs Stokes smiled. "Of
course, love," she said. "I think
Scott's right. You're the perfect
owner for Tufty, and not just
because of your hair! I know how
much you love him. I'm sure
you'll take good care of him."

"I'll be able to take Tufty to the Pet Show!" Ben said happily.

Mandy smiled at her friend. "He'll need his own cage, won't he?" she asked.

"There's a spare one in the garage," said Scott.

"Let's go and get it," said Mrs Stokes.

Mandy and Ben followed her out into the garage. There were some big cardboard boxes stacked on the shelves.

"Tufty would love these!" laughed Ben. "He could chew all day and all night!"

"We'll have to make sure he doesn't find his way in here,

then," said Mrs Stokes. "I need those boxes!"

Mandy looked around. "*There's* the cage," she said. It was sitting right on the top of the shelves.

When Mrs Stokes had lifted down the cage, Mandy and Ben cleaned it out. They filled a water bottle with fresh water and lined the floor with sawdust. They put in some empty toilet rolls for Tufty to play with.

Then they filled a little bowl with some of Scrabble's hamster mix.

"It's a pity the cage doesn't have a wheel," said Ben. "I've found this ladder for him, though."

Mandy looked at the bright blue plastic ladder. "He'll love that," she said.

Ben carefully leaned the ladder against the side of the cage, then he lifted Tufty inside.

Tufty explored every corner. Then he ran through one of the toilet rolls, and scrambled up the ladder.

"He looks really happy with his new home, Ben!" Mandy said.

On Monday morning, Mandy couldn't wait to get to school. She wanted to hear how Tufty was getting on.

She saw Ben with Richard Tanner in the playground, and ran over.

"Hi, Ben! How's Tufty?"
Mandy asked.

"He's fine, thanks," Ben
smiled. "He loves his ladder."

"We'll see him on Friday,
won't we?" Mandy asked.

"Yes," said Ben. "Would you
like to help me look after Tufty
when I bring him in?"

"I'd love to!" Mandy said.

"I wonder if he'll win a
prize?" said Ben.

Mandy thought for a
minute. "Well, lots of people
have hamsters," she said. "So
he's not an Unusual Pet."

"I don't think he'll win the
Prettiest Pet prize either," Ben said.

"He's too tufty." He grinned.

"And he doesn't have a waggy tail," Richard added.

Then Ben looked hopeful.

"Do you think Tufty might be the cleverest? He can run through toilet rolls and climb up his ladder really fast."

Richard shook his head.
"I think all hamsters do that,"
he said.

Ben looked a bit disappointed.

Mandy wanted to cheer him
up. "Never mind, Ben," she said.
"It's a shame we haven't got a
prize for the pet who looks most
like their owner. He would have
won that!"

Ben grinned, and tried to
flatten down his hair. But no –
it bounced back again, just like
Tufty's!

Chapter Five

"You're coming to school today, Mum!" Mandy said happily at breakfast time. It was Friday – Pet Show day at last!

"Make sure your mum's on her best behaviour, Mandy," said Mr Hope, winking at her.

Mandy grinned. "I will, Dad," she said. "But I'm helping Ben with Tufty, so I won't be able to watch Mum *all* the time!"

*

Class 3 was *very* different that morning! Miss Rushton had to speak very loudly as she took the register. Timmy, Peter's puppy, was barking quite a lot. Peter hung tightly on to Timmy's lead. Duchess, Richard's Persian cat, was miaowing loudly too, from inside her pet carrier.

Mandy looked over at Tufty's cage on Ben's table. "Hello, Tufty!" she whispered.

Tufty was looking out eagerly through the bars of his cage. Honey, Sally's pet rabbit, was in the next cage. Tufty climbed on to his ladder to look at her, his nose twitching.

"I think he'd like to meet all the other pets!" whispered Ben, grinning.

After registration, Mrs Hope talked to everyone about their pets, so that she could decide on the winners.

Jill told her that Toto could eat sixteen dandelions in one go! Then Gary showed Mrs Hope how smooth and dry Gertie's skin was – not slimy like most people think.

Mandy saw that Tufty had spotted Duchess. Duchess was looking very interested in Tufty. But Tufty didn't seem scared. He peered out of his cage at her and waggled his whiskers. Duchess peered back from her pet carrier, then began to purr.

"I think Tufty's found a friend, Ben!" Mandy joked.

Mandy's mum looked over to see what they were laughing about. Just then, Tufty jumped on to the bottom rung of his ladder. He rushed up to the top where he swung for a moment from one paw, then dropped down into the soft sawdust.

Mrs Hope laughed too. "He seems to be having *lots* of fun!" she said.

Ben lifted Tufty out of the cage. Straight away, Tufty ran up Ben's sleeve and on to his shoulder. The fluffy bit of fur on his head tickled Ben's neck, making him laugh again.

Mrs Hope asked Ben what he gave Tufty to eat.

Ben told her that he fed Tufty special hamster food. "And I give him fresh vegetables too, like pieces of carrot," he added.

Mrs Hope nodded. "That's good," she said. "He looks very healthy. His eyes are nice and shiny."

As she said this, Tufty ran
around the back
of Ben's neck.

"I think he wants to look at
Toto!" Mandy said. Jill's tortoise
was on the table, just behind Ben.

"He wants to be friends with
everyone," said Ben. "He's the
friendliest hamster I've ever
known!"

*

Soon it was time for the prizes to be given out. Mandy couldn't wait to find out who had won!

First of all, Mrs Hope announced the prize for the Waggiest Tail. The winner was Timmy, of course! Timmy wagged his tail faster than ever as Peter collected his big red rosette.

Next came the Prettiest Pet. "It was very difficult to decide," Mrs Hope said. "All of your pets are pretty! But in the end I picked Honey, Sally's pet rabbit. She has such lovely silky fur."

Sally beamed, and pinned Honey's rosette on her pet carrier.

"And now for the Cleverest Pet," said Mrs Hope. "When Richard reminded me about

Duchess's painting, she had to be the winner!"

Mandy grinned. Duchess had once joined in Class 3's Art lesson, and she'd had her paw-print paintings pinned on the wall!

"So Duchess is the Cleverest Pet," said Mrs Hope.

Richard hugged Duchess, grinning happily.

Now there was just one prize left.

"Finally, the Most Unusual Pet," said Mrs Hope.

Mandy looked around. It had to be either Toto the tortoise or Gertie the garter snake, she decided. But she was wrong!

"Woody and Twig, Will's stick insects!" Mrs Hope announced.

As Will went to collect his
rosette, Ben stroked Tufty's fur.
"I knew Tufty wouldn't get a
prize," he whispered to Mandy.

"Never mind," Mandy
whispered back. "He's still lovely."

Ben smiled and nodded.

Then Miss Rushton said,
"I've found an extra rosette.
Would you like to choose who it
should go to, Mrs Hope?"

Mandy held her breath.
Which pet would her mum
choose?

Mrs Hope looked round the
class and smiled. She seemed to
be thinking very hard.

"Well . . ." she said at last.

"It's been lovely to see so many happy, healthy pets. I wish I could give a prize to everyone. But there's one pet that really made me smile. The prize goes to Tufty, for being the Happiest Pet!"

Everyone clapped extra loud. Ben went bright red with delight. He tried to smooth down his hair, then collected his rosette from Mrs Hope.

Mandy thought this was the *perfect* end to the Pet Show. "I think there should be one more prize," she joked, as Ben came back to the table. "For Ben – the Happiest Owner!"

Chapter One

"I think I'm going to melt, Grandad!" Mandy Hope said. "It's so *hot*." She looked up at the blue sky. It was the first week of the summer holidays, and it felt like the sun had been shining for ever.

Grandad Hope stopped digging and wiped his brow. "We'll be finished soon," he said. "There's not much more to do."

Mandy was helping her grandad to clear a patch of garden at Animal Ark, where she lived. Her mum and dad were very busy at work, and Grandad Hope loved gardening so he had offered to help out.

Just then Mandy's mum came out carrying her vet's bag.

"Mandy, I'm going to Appletree Cottage," she called. "Do you want to come with me?"

Mandy dropped her armful of weeds into the wheelbarrow and brushed the front of her T-shirt. Her mum had visited Appletree Cottage before. "That's where Mr and Mrs Henderson live," she said. "And they've got lots of animals."

"You'd better go with your Mum, then!" Grandad Hope laughed.

Mandy was mad about animals. Her mum and dad were both vets. There were always lots of animals around, and that was just the way Mandy liked it.

"Are you sure you don't mind, Grandad?" Mandy asked.

Grandad Hope shook his head. "No, of course not," he said. "Off you go, love."

"Don't work too hard," Mandy's mum said to Grandad. "It's much too hot."

Grandad smiled and nodded. "But I like digging!" he said. He picked up his spade again. "See you later."

Mrs Hope and Mandy went out to the car.

"Why are we going to Appletree Cottage, Mum?" Mandy asked. "Is one of the animals sick?"

"No," replied her mum. "The Hendersons have gone on holiday, and someone else is looking after the animals. Mrs Henderson asked if I would visit to see if they need any advice."

"Who is looking after the animals?" Mandy wanted to know.

"Mr Henderson's sister, Mrs Ford," said Mrs Hope. "And her children, Emma and Ellie."